The Hedgerow Circus

Written by Ruth Thomson
Illustrated by Jolyne Knox

PUBLISHED BY THE READER'S DIGEST ASSOCIATION LIMITED

It was Midsummer's Eve.
All seemed quiet in the hedgerow,
but there was magic in the air.

The ants scurried here and there.

The beetles skittered and scuttled.

The bees buzzed back and forth.

The butterflies flitted and fluttered.

The hedgehogs sniffed
and snuffled.

The birds cheeped
and twittered.

At last everything was ready.
The stage was set.
The feast was laid.

The hedgerow circus was about
to begin.
"Roll up! Roll up!" called
the ringmaster, dressed smartly
in a spotted coat.
Everybody gathered around
the stage.
"Let the show begin!"

The grasshoppers were first.
The smallest one leaped
on to the middle of the stage.
"Aah," said everyone.
The middle one leaped
almost to the far edge.
"Ooh," said everyone.

The largest grasshopper of all
jumped all the way over the stage
and landed on the other side.
"Wow," said everyone, clapping
loudly.
"Who's next?" asked the harvest
mouse.

"It's my turn," said the spider,
twirling round and round
on his thread, lowering himself
at great speed.
"Watch this!"
This way and that he swung,
up and down, round and round,
making a web before everyone's
very eyes.
The audience cheered.

The spider sat proudly
in the middle of his web
and took a bow.
"Who's next?" asked the harvest
mouse.

"Are we next?"
shouted the hedgehogs.

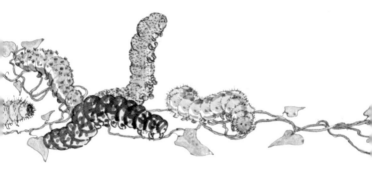

"No," said the ringmaster,
"It's time for the tug-of-war."
The caterpillars twined themselves
round the bindweed stalk
and got ready to pull.
"Wait," called the ringmaster,

"We've forgotten the line."
The snail had an idea.
She slowly crept her way forward
leaving a thin slimy line behind
her, right between the two teams.

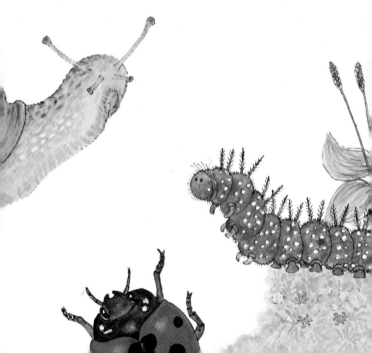

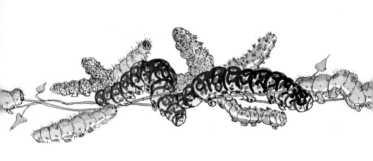

"Right," said the blackbird,
who was acting as referee,
"Are you ready to begin?
On your marks, get set, go!"

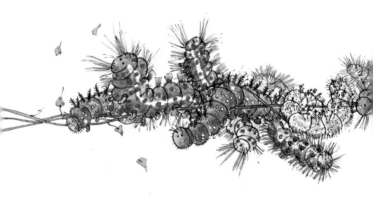

The caterpillars pulled
with all their might.
First one way
and then the other.
Who was going to win?

It seemed an even match,
but all of a sudden,
the peacock caterpillar lost
his grip.
The hairy caterpillars
were tugged over the line
and fell together into a heap.
The audience clapped wildly.

"Who's next?" asked the harvest mouse.

"Is it our turn?" the hedgehogs
asked again.

"Not yet," said the ringmaster
firmly. "Now it's time
for the butterfly dance."
The butterflies, who had been
quietly feeding on the flowers,
rose silently up
above the hedgerow.

Higher and higher they flew,
darting and fluttering
in the warm, still air.
Their colours glowed
in the evening sunshine.
"How beautiful," chorused
everyone.

"Who's next?" asked the
harvest mouse.
"You're next," said the ringmaster.
The harvest mouse turned pale,
but hurried over
to the nearest stalk
and climbed up.

"Look at me," he cried,
nimbly jumping from one stalk
to another, using his tail
to help him.
Everybody watched open-mouthed.

"Us next?" asked the impatient
hedgehogs.
The ringmaster shook his head.
"The shrews are going to do
their trick next."
Two shrews came on to the stage
and bowed to the audience.

"I'm going to hide," said one.
"And I'm going to find him,"
said the other.

The second shrew shut his eyes . . .

whilst the first one jumped
into the audience and crouched
behind a wren.
The shrew on the stage
opened his eyes.
First he sniffed the air . . .

then he sniffed the ground
and walked towards the wren.
"There," he said, pointing
triumphantly, and up popped
the hidden shrew.

"And now," said the ringmaster,
"it's the hedgehogs' turn."
The audience waited eagerly.
But what was that?

Clomp! Stomp! Clomp! Stomp!
Clomp! Stomp! Clomp! Stomp!
Noisy thuds came closer and closer.

"Run!" shouted the ringmaster.
"Hide!" squealed the harvest mouse.
The animals scattered.

They held their breath
and closed their eyes.

Clomp!
Down came one very large,
very muddy gumboot.

Stomp!
Down came another very large,
very muddy gumboot.

Clomp, stomp! Clomp, stomp!
Clomp, clump.
The footsteps faded away.
Everyone opened their eyes.
They hardly dared to look.
"Oh no," squeaked the hedgehogs,
"The stage is squashed to bits."

"But our feast is all right,"
twittered the birds.
"Hooray!" cheered everybody.
"Time to eat."

By the gleam of the glow-worms
everyone feasted . . .

until they could eat no more.

And the hedgehogs had their turn
after all!

MY NATURE LIBRARY

First Edition Copyright © 1982
The Reader's Digest Association
Limited, Berkeley Square House,
Berkeley Square, London W1X 6AB
Reprinted 1991

® READER'S DIGEST, THE DIGEST and
the Pegasus logo are registered trademarks of
The Reader's Digest Association, Inc.
of Pleasantville, New York, U.S.A.

Phototypeset by Tradespools Limited
Frome, Somerset.
Printed in Hong Kong

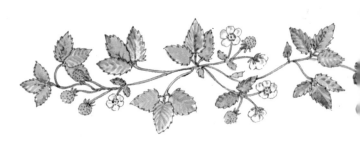